Dove Tales

ROBERT DAVID BURRIS

ISBN 978-1-64140-601-7 (paperback)
ISBN 978-1-64140-602-4 (digital)

Christian Faith Publishing, Inc.
832 Park Avenue
Meadville, PA 16335
www.christianfaithpublishing.com

Printed in the United States of America

Dedicated to:

Dear Lamb,

Remember Always Look for the Dove in every story.

Blessings,

Robert D. Burris

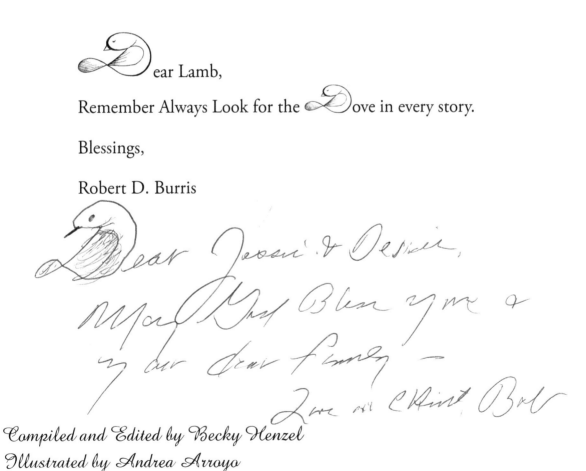

Compiled and Edited by Becky Henzel
Illustrated by Andrea Arroyo
Contributing Illustrators: _____

Foreword

The dedication page challenges the child to "always look for the 'Dove' [meaning the Christ-Spirit] in every story." The Tales are intentionally not preachy but are meant to convey the subtleties of our Lord's character and ministry features with a strong emphasis on redemptive parody. The illustrations are original by Ms. Andrea Arroyo. The structure is designed with paper stock dividers between the tales for use to help parents suggest illustrations to their children of a feature of the tale; a character(s), human or not; or a behavior being illustrated. Once the child illustrates something in each of the stories, there is a spot on the dedication page for them to add their name(s) as co-illustrators. Then the work can be given as a keepsake to a grandmother or father or whoever as an emblem of their child's or grandchild's understanding of the true lantent gospel narrative. This will have the further benefit of blessing them as well.

Three of the stories are drawn from real-life incidences in my very youth. Dove Tales is meant to be interactive between parents and children; those children from four to seven years of age.

CONTENTS

The Tale of Paddy, the Lame Duck

The lagoon sure was busy this day. It seemed as if everyone was there, either swimming or playing tag or diving off rocks and lily pads.

There was Weaver the beaver and his brothers gathering materials for a dam they were building. Groggy the frog was playing leap frog with Seagrin the grasshopper. Doc the Stork was there with many new animals as well. Newly arrived to the lagoon was a beautiful blue-green-brown-purple-pink-hazel heron named Kevin, who was eagerly pecking at the clumps of bodie bodie seagrass bordering the shoreline and doing all this while balancing on his one and only leg. Lizzy the lizard was sunning herself on a rock. And a school of goldfish was having a lesson on water safety.

Professor Gandy, the oldest goose in the pond, was there too, telling stories to anyone who would listen about how the pond used to be before it had gotten so crowded. Everyone knew each other, and soon, even the new animals were warmly welcomed by all.

This is the story of a little duck name Paddy and his brothers and sisters. Now Paddy was not a normal duck, you see. For even though he had very large webbed feet, still he could not waddle on land or swim in water. He could not use his legs at all. This meant that everywhere his brothers and sisters went they had to carry Paddy along with them. They could not leave him alone. So they each took turns watching him.

One time they had tried putting Paddy in the water, thinking he would surely be able to float around a little. But he soon lost his balance and turned upside down. When he couldn't get upright again, he almost drowned.

Babysitting Paddy made his brothers and sisters resentful because it always meant that one of them would not be able to participate in the water relays or other activities of the lagoon. And Paddy was embarrassed by having to be carried everywhere he went. And he was sad in knowing he was causing his family to miss out on all the fun.

The other animals knew about Paddy, but none seemed to want him as a friend. After all, a duck who couldn't walk or swim wouldn't be much fun. So they just ignored him.

This day was a glorious day however. Everyone, young and old, was at the pond. Paddy asked to be set down right alongside the water's edge. He told his brothers and sisters to all go and have a good time—that he would be alright. After much coaxing, they left Paddy by himself near the water's edge.

Just then, Segrin the grasshopper took a flying double flip, topsy-turvy, over the back somersault leap off a small bush frond two and a half feet from the water, making a slight splash. Everyone laughed and clapped their wings, fins, and paws, very surprised at his dive. All the animals, that is, except Paddy, who was watching the water's surface very, vveerryy carefully because he had seen something unusual moving in the water. It was a long brown line riding just beneath the water's surface. He had never seen this large of an animal before in the pond. And he felt he had better try and see what it was.

He quickly tucked himself into a ball, rocked forward, and rolled down into the water. As usual, he was upside down, but when he opened his eyes, he saw a large alligator coming toward him and his family and others in the pond.

Paddy started to quack up. He quacked and quacked, louder and louder, until everyone was alerted to the unfriendly alligator and hurried to get out of the pond. Then his brothers and sisters paddled over to Paddy and pulled him out of the water to safety.

When the unfriendly alligator could not find anyone left in the pond to eat, he finally left. And all the animals breathed a sigh of relief. They all rushed over to thank Paddy and tell him how grateful they were to him for risking his life to warn them about the alligator.

The next day, before Paddy arrived at the pond, Groggy the frog gathered all the animals together and told them his idea, and they took up a collection. They went into the village to talk with Herr Rabbit, the German cobbler.

Groggy the frog told Herr Rabbit about Paddy and asked him if he could build something that would allow Paddy to go into the pond without drowning.

The following week, all the animals were again assembled at the pond. Then came Paddy being pulled by his brothers and sisters on what looked like a skateboard with pontoons stemming out on either side. On each pontoon was written the word "LIFEGUARD." They easily pulled him down and into the pond where the pontoons took over to hold him upright in the water.

A swan who was new to the pond asked, "Is that the lame duck everyone's been talking about?"

Just then, Groggy the frog jumped up on a lily pad and said, "That's no lame duck! That's Paddy. He's our lifeguard. He's the wisest quacker in the whole pond."

"And the loudest too," added Weaver the beaver. "And he's our friend."

The Tale of Paddy, the Lame Duck

Did you find the 'DOVE' in the Tale?

The Tale of Paddy,
the Lame Duck

Did you find the 'DOVE' in the Tale?

W h a t   L i t t l e   H o u s e k e e p e r s   D o !

It is important to have adventures at play
of lions and monkeys and tigers.
But important too are the things you do,
to make Mom's job go lighter.
Each taking a turn to get the work done,
and knowing a burden you're bearing
is important as the games you play
and fun you may be sharing.
To be a help to Mom each day
and seeing she's never neglected.
Here's a list of things Little Housekeepers might do,
And all have been carefully selected.

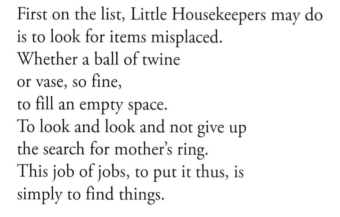

First on the list, Little Housekeepers may do
is to look for items misplaced.
Whether a ball of twine
or vase, so fine,
to fill an empty space.
To look and look and not give up
the search for mother's ring.
This job of jobs, to put it thus, is
simply to find things.

Next on the list, Little Housekeepers may do,
is not generally expected.
But those who are wise will take time to see
That Mom's wish is usually respected.

Please keep the door
of the refrigerator shut tight,
whenever you're about it.
The object is this,
and one not to be missed,
to keep the cool air in
and the warm air out it.

Sometimes Little Housekeepers find the greatest of joys
in playing with bears and other stuffed toys.
But when it comes time to put them away,
an argument starts and Mother's will holds sway.
But wouldn't it be nice
if just once in a while
you put your own toys away,
and did so with a smile?
Then would you be a good Little Housekeeper,
In doing your chores
and taking care of things that are yours.

Sometimes Little Housekeepers help
to water the household plants.
But this is hardly a job to be done
that mommies may leave to chance.
For if you mistake and water too much
or give too much tender care
then next watering time, a surprise you may find,
limbs once filled with leaves are now bare.

Early in the morning into the kitchen they creep
assembling pots and pans with nary a peep.
They grab for the peanut butter, jelly, and bread,
all to make mother breakfast in bed.
Soon the effort is over; the spillage at last,
Mother sits up and is slightly aghast
To see a large glass of chocolate milk

on a tray piled high with peanut butter paste.
She looks at her child;
her face filled with a smile,
and thinks once or twice about taking a taste.

Finally, she does, and the moment of truth is had,
The gift is accepted, and it isn't half-bad.
For mother at least, her kitchen a mess,
will mean apron and glove.
But for the Little Housekeeper, Mom knows,
this breakfast she chose
was a wonderful gift of her love.

Many Little Housekeepers, even though they may be small,
are sometimes asked to do things
for which one must be tall—
close the curtains, dust the bureau,
and turn off the light in your room.
Out comes a stool to stand upon; be careful not to swoon.
Safety first! And be careful too!
Little Housekeepers hear mommies preach.
But to use a stool around the house is a rule
for things just out of reach.

To hear a call from a friend outdoors
can sometimes exceed fondest wishes.
But just when so inclined,
as if reading your mind,
Mother will yell, "We're ready now to do dishes."
So with apron affixed;
and soap and water well mixed,
the Little Housekeeper begins without speech.
For her job can be seen
to get the dishes so clean,
so that nothing is heard but a squeak.

Sometimes Little Housekeepers help,
by telling time of day.
For mommies who are running late
it is an important way,
of helping Mommy tend to things
and see the word get done,
by running to the clock yourself
and telling her: the big hand's on five,
and the little hand's on one.
So when Mommy gets too busy,
Or whenever she asks of you,
if you would just let her know that:
the big hand's pointing to six
and the little hand's pointing to two.

Down on your hands! And down on your knees
to get slippers from under the bed.
It is better for Mommy to ask
a Little Housekeeper to do this, instead.
Down on the floor, and flat on your tummy,
to find glasses rolled under the table,
for mommies have learned this job must be spurned.
Besides, Little Housekeepers are far more able,
to go down into a squat, almost tied in a knot,
and fetch things pushed under the couch,
is an advantage enjoyed by little girls and boys,
who can see everything from a crouch.

As evening draws near
the dinner dishes all cleared,
and the housework for the day almost done,
the Little Housekeeper is keen
to peel off blouse and jeans
and take a flying leap into the tub.
First in goes the soap, then scuffy tugboat
and finally her small rubber duck.

When at last she is seen
The fact that she's clean,
is a sight, less by design than of luck.

Now, by these examples here told,
I hope it's been shown:
a Little Housekeeper's job from morning 'til evening
is responsibility shared
by Little Housekeepers who care,
and Mommy's appreciation receiving.
So I offer to you these suggestions not new,
But please give them proper inspection.
And maybe if you have thought of others to do,
you may add these to your collection.

What Little Housekeepers Do!

Did you find the 'DOVE' in the Tale?

What Little Housekeepers Do!

Did you find the 'DOVE' in the Tale?

Kamal's Night Journey

"Hurry up! Get up! Up! Hurry!" Kamal opened his eyes and felt Blawal tapping gently with a stick on his front and back legs. He wondered what all the excitement and rush was about, seeing as it was still the middle of the night.

But he soon learned that he was to be laden with food and blankets and supplies sufficient for what only could be a very long desert journey. As he stood listening to his master and Blawal talk, he heard Caspar say something about the appearance of a very large star.

Now this interested Kamal very much. But when they began to strap supplies to his back and cinch the straps under his stomach, he got very angry. To be awakened out of a sound sleep was one thing. But to be burdened down with supplies for a long journey in the dead of night was more than this camel's patience could take.

He didn't like the desert much during the daytime. But he disliked traveling at night through the desert even more. There would be the million potholes along the well-traveled caravan roads. And he knew that he would probably step into every one of them. And he also disliked the wind storms because they would blow dust and sand into his nose and eyes, making it even more difficult to stay on the roads.

When all was ready, Caspar led him out of his stable and onto the road where he saw his two friends, Ronak and Sumbal. They, too, were burdened down with many supplies. Kamal was glad to see that he would have some company at least—someone to complain to that would understand his feelings about their journey.

He moved closer to his friends to share his anger with them and to get some more details about their trip. As he did, he saw Ronak's master open a scroll and utter the word "Bethlehem." He saw Caspar nod his head and point his finger high toward the western sky. Then all three lifted their heads and stood in silence, gazing at the most unusual sight. Kamal saw it too—in the distance—a star so bright and whose beams of light so long that it appeared to pointing to a certain spot on the desert's horizon.

Kamal would admit to his friends that he was mildly excited about the star. And being a fairly adventurous camel, he wondered what it could mean. But he still resented being awakened in the middle of the night, for he felt he had earned his eight hours of rest and now he was being cheated out of them.

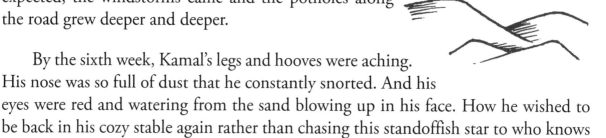

Not long after the journey had begun, it became clear to all that the star was moving with them. And by its long beams of light was pointing to a spot on the horizon the star seemed to be directing them to move. But the star would not get any closer. And just as Kamal had expected, the windstorms came and the potholes along the road grew deeper and deeper.

By the sixth week, Kamal's legs and hooves were aching. His nose was so full of dust that he constantly snorted. And his eyes were red and watering from the sand blowing up in his face. How he wished to be back in his cozy stable again rather than chasing this standoffish star to who knows where.

Two weeks earlier Kamal had recognized some other camels with the east-west trade caravan stopped at one of the desert springs. He had hoped that his master and other traveling companions would pull close enough and stop for a visit or purchase some supplies. He loved to chew the fat with these worldly camels because they always had the best stories to tell. Their stories were always fresh and exciting to hear. But as they turned away from the caravan, Kamal realized that Caspar intended to let nothing prevent him from following the star. And so Kamal knew that a long uninterrupted journey lay in front of him and that he might as well make the best of it.

Kamal stopped complaining so much and started thinking more about the star. He wondered what it could mean and where it was leading them. He had heard his master and his friend talk over and over again about a town called Bethlehem. He had heard King Melchior mention the words "prophesy" and "scripture." But when king

Balthazar spoke of a "deliverer," everyone sat quiet and wondered. And no more words were spoken again that night.

As Kamal's attitude improved, he began to think how really honored a camel he was. He knew his master was one of the wisest and richest men in their city. Important people in the town were always asking his advice about government or crop-planting and the heavens, about which Caspar was considered an expert. He also knew anything King Caspar considered important enough to do would not be boring or uneventful for very long.

In this judgment, Kamal was correct. For on the second day of the eighth week of their journey, as the long night's travel was ending and the day was beginning to dawn, the Star grew very faint, and they could see the outline of a large city on the horizon. Balthazar called the city Jerusalem. The night following was to be one that Kamal would never forget.

As evening drew near, they had just started traveling when they noticed the star was getting larger and also closer. To them, it appeared to be hovering over or near the great city. Kamal, Ronak, and Sumbal were excited to see that their long journey was finally ending in this very large city. And they thought and talked about warm stables and fresh hay. They talked about having good conversation with the other camels and even of racing with some of the local mules.

As they approached the gate of Jerusalem, they were puzzled to see that the Star still lay outside the city, just over the next rise. It was then that Caspar realized Bethlehem was to be their final destination that night, even as he had read from the scroll.

From the ridge, they looked down on the little town of Bethlehem lying peaceful and still. And saw the Star had stationed itself just over a small stable attached to the rear of an inn. As they slowly came closer to the stable, they saw a herd of sheep and goats standing quietly with their shepherds before the entrance. They saw no torches, no lanterns—only the Star gave them its light.

Just outside the stable, Kamal bent his front legs low so his master could get down. He looked around to see that Ronak and Sumbal had already settled themselves down on the cool grass to wait. He was amazed that after so long a journey, they could act so disinterested in everything taking place. He craned his neck as hard as he could to see into the stable. He was able to get a glimpse of a young woman seated on a mound of hay and cradling a very young child on her lap.

Then suddenly, Kamal gasped! For he saw something happen that he thought he would never see and that did not make any sense to him at all. He watched his master, along with King Melchior and King Balthazar each in turn quietly kneel down before the woman and child and offer them gold, frankincense, and myrrh. He watched Caspar fold his arms and hands together, close his eyes, and softly whisper something to the child before him.

Kamal had seen other men pay homage and respect in this way to kings in their palaces and courtyards. But never before had he seen this reverence paid to a child of such humble beginnings.

He asked a ram standing near if he knew what all these things meant. The ram told him of the heavenly vision of angels and their message to the shepherds to go quickly to Bethlehem. And there to see One, born a Savior, Who is Christ, the Son of the Most High. There they would see the Deliverer promised of old, who would free all men from their sins.

Kamal's heart was pounding. He slowly settled himself down on the cool grass and closed his eyes. He was not tired, and he did not sleep. He just knew that it was now time to be quiet. In the quiet waiting, Kamal felt warm and peaceful inside. He wondered why he had been chosen to bear this man, Caspar, as a messenger of peace and welcome to the Son of the Most High God.

His thoughts came very fast now and were often a bit jumbled. He remembered something that he had heard his master say many years ago: "That, in the vast barrenness of the desert; in the rush of the mighty winds that blow, and in the clearness of the evening desert sky, one could learn something of the power and greatness of the

Creator." But as Kamal now looked upon this Child, he knew that he was learning something too of the love of that Creator.

Yes, Kamal now had a story to tell that would need to be retold over and over again—a story ever fresh and exciting to hear.

Kamal's Night Journey

Did you find the 'DOVE' in the Tale?

Did you find the 'DOVE' in the Tale?

A Trip through the Zoo
or an Animal Stew

To see Monkeys swinging
Maybe Seals singing
Or an Alligator grinning at you.
These things will be found
Whether in midair or on ground
On a wonderful trip through the zoo.

To see a Fat Turkey trot
Or a Cock-On-The-Walk.
And hear occasional cock-a-doodle-doos.
The Whooping Cranes with lamenting refrains
Are sounds only heard at the zoo.

To see Long-Necked giraffes
Or hear Hyenas laugh
Or see a slightly Bow-Legged Egret
Are sights waiting for you,
A regular animal stew
And one you will never forget.

So come along on our trip
And see these great gifts,
The unfolding of God's wonderful design,
As His care will appear
For these creatures so dear
That will surely stick in your mind.

Our first stop to be made
Before a large wire cage
Is to see a Saucy Green Parrot
With feathers so sleek
And large nut-cracking beak
And eyes the color of claret:
"Speak little parrot
Speak if you will,
Surely some words are in order,"
For God has planned
To be a mimic of man
This green-feathered tape recorder.

I'm sure you'll agree
This next animal we see
Is among the oddest of all in the park.
Here clearly is shown,
(And God's sense of humor made known),
By the wonderful Long-Nosed Aardvark.
With sense of smell so keen,
His food he will glean
This remarkable insect-eater.
But take a closer look and you'll see,
And with imagination there'll be
A four-legged vacuum cleaner.

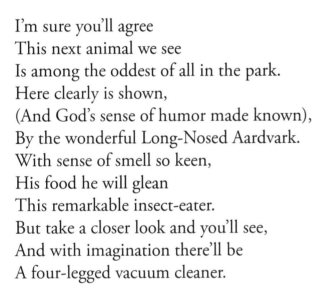

The next act to follow
Is one hard to swallow
For a bird not very graceful in flight.
Swooping low for a catch
Fast fishes to snatch
Then soars up again to new heights.
I'm sure you've been told
In true storybook fashion
That the Stork is really a Pelican.
But I'm sure you've not learned

From a hunting trip returned
That his beak will hold more
Than his belly can.

The next animal fare
Is a Big Grizzly Bear
Whose name happens to be Chester.
Motion as if you were king
His obedience it will bring
And he will become your court jester.
He'll roll on the ground
Or stand upside down
Your next royal command he's awaiting—
But when you are through
He'll expect a cookie or two
As ample reward, if I'm not mistaken.
But do you see those long claws
Extending down from his paws?
This playfulness is not all it seems.
For if it ever came down
To coming face-to-face with our clown
I hope it would be just in a dream.

It would take a long time
The right words to combine
To picture our next animal clearly.
Its design at first glance
(And not one left to chance)
Blends with God's sense of humor so surely.
With legs like tree trunks
But forepaws preshrunk
And a back rolled into a slouch.
So take time to treasure
In word rhymes to measure
A treat God has planned just for you.
Come along and we'll share

This animal so rare—
The Jumping Jack Kangaroo!

Our next ingredient too
For our tasty animal stew
Is the Bleary-Eyed Hippopotamus.
Be alert and you'll learn
Some things about him
That are not usually taught to us.
After a big meal
The urge he will feel,
The company of this world to shun.
He'll go into the slough
For an hour or two
Then rise up again looking for lunch;
But don't be so bold
With criticism too cold
For this behavior so monotonous.
Just stop and reflect these deeds we reject
Are often done by a lot of us.

A problem here posed (and don't laugh)
Concerning the Long-Necked Giraffe
With head in treetops
Where cool breezes won't stop
And his nose always caught in a draft!
Now if this doesn't serious sound
I ask that you please stay around.
For if he should sneeze
While his head's in the trees
It will scatter his food to the ground.
So the problem into which he's been cast
Our friend will now be forced to fast
For how to get down to his food on the ground
Is difficult for a Two-Story Giraffe.

The last stop to be made
on our animal parade
To see are Monkeys who truly like to tease.
They'll hang limb from limb
Your attention to win,
Then glide through the air as if on a trapeze.
Their faces so charming,
Their antics disarming,
Each moment of play they will seize.
With arms outstretched, hoping
For peanuts and fruit, groping,
Then off again to do just as they please…

Lions and Tigers and Penguins and Elk,
Camels with one hump or two,
Lil Phoebes, up on the wing
Fleet-Footed Gazelles,
Slow Turtles in their shells
Form part of our animal stew.
So lest you feel Cheetah-ed
By a recipe not completed
There's a Ram standing by a Woolly Ewe.
The Zebra of course
Is just a Striped Horse
(so what else is "GNU"?)

There are many more seasonings too
That belong in an animal stew.
But for lack of space
I can only give you this taste
Of a wonderful trip through
the zoo.

Z
O
A TRIP THROUGH
H
E
OR.........
AN

S
T
E
W

Did you find the 'DOVE' in the Tale?

A Trip through the Zoo
or an Animal Stew

Did you find the 'DOVE' in the Tale?

A Wheelchair, a Dog, and Friends

Holly, too, could feel the excitement for the big Easter Day picnic and contest approaching. As she looked down from her bedroom window, she could see the neighborhood children scampering about in the street below.

She knew they had all entered the big contest planned by the town for the Easter Day celebration. And she could see they were busily gathering ribbons, streamers, and balloons with which to decorate their entries. (You see, the contest rules stated that the children could enter anything they wanted as long as it was on wheels and that a trophy would be awarded for the most original and brightly colored entry.)

Holly could see Johnny next door weaving ribbons in and out of the spokes of his bicycle and tying streamers to the handlebars. She could see Leila across the street painting her bicycle too and her lil' sis Mary, tying a big bow on her dolly carriage. She knew that Georgie down the street would enter his one-wheel unicycle and that others were entering their skateboards.

Holly could see and feel the excitement expressed by the children as she lay watching from her bed. But the longer she watched, the sadder and lonelier she began to feel. For since the Henzels had moved into town three months earlier, Holly had not made any new friends. She knew she could not enter the upcoming contest. And that she would probably spend the day of the picnic either lying in bed or sitting on the front porch, in her wheelchair, alone.

One day, shortly after Holly had first moved into the neighborhood, she had been sitting on her front porch when Johnny, Leila, Sarah, Mathew, Joshua, Cho Cho, lil' sis Mary, and Georgie all came over to say hello and to see her wheelchair. It was then she had tried to tell them about the accident she had been in when she was four years old and how she could no longer move her legs. When they found out Holly could not run or jump or ride bicycles or play tag with them, they did not offer to include her in any of their games. Finally, they stopped coming over to see her at all. They didn't even say hello when they saw her sitting on the porch; they just pretended she wasn't there.

However, Holly was not always alone, for Johnny's dog, Alex Van Wiggle-Woggle, would always come over to play fetch-the-stick with her. Johnny had nicknamed Alex "Mr. Van Wiggle-Woggle" because whenever he was petted or played with, he would wiggle and woggle his tail and rear end so hard that one thought he was going to split in two. He loved to play fetch-the-stick with Holly because she would throw the stick for him for hours. Whereas the other children would only toss it once or twice and then would get tired and quit to do something different.

When there was no one around to play fetch-the-stick with, Alex had another game that he played by himself. He would push his stick as far as he could under the wire fence that separated Holly's and Johnny's houses and then lunge as hard as he could, burrowing his head, neck, shoulders, and front legs under the fence while scratching and clawing at the stick, trying to retrieve it. He would do this over and over, pushing the stick a little farther under the fence each time.

Holly loved to watch him play this game. She would laugh and howl and clap for him each time he retrieved the stick. Sometimes all she would see for a long time was his tail and rear end wiggling and "woggling" back and forth. It was a very funny sight. In this way, Holly passed the time without thinking how lonely she was to be without friends.

The afternoon before the contest was strangely quiet. Holly was sitting on her front porch in her wheelchair, alone. From there she could see Johnny's mother through her kitchen window. And she could smell the wonderful cookies she was baking to take to the picnic the next day. Johnny and Leila and Georgie had not yet come home from school. And she had just finished a long game of fetch-the-stick with Alex.

Suddenly, there was a very loud yip and howl followed by a low whimpering and then another half-bark and gasp followed by more whimpering. Holly was startled and shivered in her chair. She looked over to see that Alex had his head and shoulders and front legs caught in the wire fence and how entangled he was becoming. She saw the cuts around his neck made by the barbed wire. And she could see that he was gasping for air.

Holly knew she must try to free him before he choked. She wheeled her chair as close as she could to the edge of the porch steps. But as she did, the chair's wheels skidded off the porch, throwing her down onto the grassy lawn and her chair half-leaning against the shrub down next to the porch.

Holly was only a few feet away from Alex so she began to pull herself along the ground using just her arms. She finally reached the poor dog and was able to get a hand on one of the wires on which he was caught. She had a hard time freeing him though because his tail kept wiggling and woggling in her face. This made her nose itch, and she had to stop her rescue attempt twice in order to scratch it. Finally, she was able to free Alex from the fence.

Just then, Johnny, Leila, and Georgie came yelling and running up for they had heard Alex's cry for help halfway down the street. Johnny's mother heard the children's screams, and she too came running over to see if Holly was all right.

Miss Holly Henzel lay on the ground bruised and cut and panting for the excitement with Alex trying to lick her face.

Johnny knelt down next to Alex, hugged his neck, and said what a good dog he was and that he would bandage his cuts. Johnny's mother went and got Mrs. Henzel, and together they carried Holly up to her bed where they tended her bruised arms and bandaged the cuts on her hands.

When Johnny had finished trying to put salve and bandages on Alex's wounds, getting salve in his own eyes four times and gluing his eyelashes shut; he ran out the front door and over to see the place in the fence where Alex had been caught. As he looked through the fence, he saw Holly's wheelchair still leaning against the bush where it had fallen.

He slowly walked over to the Henzel's front yard and picked up the wheelchair. After he set the chair back upright on the porch, he straightened a bent spoke in one of the wheels, brushed off the seat, and sat down.

As Johnny sat in the wheelchair, he thought. He thought about his dog, Alex, and how he almost died. He thought about the picnic the next day and his decorated bicycle that he would ride in the contest. And for the first time, sitting in her chair, he thought about Holly Henzel.

Suddenly, he jumped up and pounded on the Henzels' front door. When Mrs. Henzel opened the door, he quickly whispered something in her ear and then ran over to his own house. He threw open the door, ran into the kitchen where his mother was, and excitedly whispered something in her ear. He then raced out the front door, leaving it open behind him, and went and told Leila and Georgie his plan.

The following day began as usual for Holly. Her father had come up to her room, picked her up, and started to carry her downstairs. Halfway down the stairs, he stopped. Holly looked up and was startled to see Georgie, Leila, Johnny, and Alex all standing in a semicircle around the most beautifully and gaily decorated wheelchair she had ever seen.

Holly began to cry, for she recognized the colored ribbons woven in between the wheel spokes and the streamers tied to the arms were the same ones Johnny had used to decorate his bicycle. Johnny said that he would not be entering his bicycle this year, but that he was going to be in the contest, pushing Holly Henzel in her wheelchair.

The next afternoon, the contest finally began, and everyone in town was now seated on the bleachers, anxiously awaiting the children to begin parading their entries before the contest judges. The children were lined up in a long wide arc, one behind the other, with Holly and Johnny in front. The word was given to begin the parade.

As the procession of children and bicycles wound around before the judges, everyone clapped and shouted or whistled as their child came into view. It was a glorious sight to see the many colored banners and ribbons and to see the work the children had put into each entry. After all had been seen, the judges announced that the first prize for the most original and brightly decorated entry would go to Miss Holly Henzel, and they awarded to her the beautiful trophy.

Everyone clapped and shouted their approval. Leila, Georgie, Sarah, Mathew, Joshua, Cho Cho and lil' sis Mary all hurried over to hug Holly and congratulate her. Just then, Alex Van Wiggle-Woggle, with his stick in his mouth, pulled loose from the leash Johnny's father had been holding him with and bounded out of the grandstand toward Holly. He put his front paws up on the arm of her chair and dropped his stick into her lap.

Holly was glad for the trophy, for she had never before won anything. She was glad for Alex's stick on her lap, and for the first time, she was even glad for her wheelchair. But above everything else, Holly was the happiest for her newly won friends. And she knew that she would never be lonely again.

A Wheelchair, A Dog, and Friends

Did you find the 'DOVE' in the Tale?

A Wheelchair, a Dog, and Friends

Did you find the 'DOVE' in the Tale?

Planting a Tree for Gramma

As Father came down the stairs, he saw Rebecca sitting at the breakfast table, trying to get Crystal, her dolly, to eat. She had her doll propped up on three pillows and was trying to push a large spoonful of oatmeal into her mouth, most of which was landing on the floor.

"That's good, Crystal!" she said. "Eat it all up and you can have a cookie."

Father walked over to the breakfast table and sat down, still grinning at his daughter's make-believe mothering. But his smile soon disappeared when Mother entered the room and with a scowl on her face exclaimed, "How did all this oatmeal get on the floor?"

"Well, Mommy, I was just feeding Crystal her breakfast, and she wouldn't eat it, and so she spit up it on the floor."

Her mother nodded her head, looked at her father who was trying to stifle a grin, and told Rebecca to get a paper towel and clean the cereal off the rug.

They all as a family had just sat down to breakfast together when Mother asked if Father had given some thought about what to get Grandma for her birthday. But before he could answer, Rebecca charged back into the room, carrying the whole roll of paper towels. "Can I come too Daddy and buy Gramma's present?"

"Of course you can!" said Father.

Mother suggested a new tablecloth or dishware. But Father said he wanted to get Grandma something she didn't already have and that she wouldn't buy for herself. Rebecca, popping her head up from wiping the rug, said, "I know what Gramma needs. She needs a dolly like my Crystal so she won't be lonely! And I will pick one for her special."

At this, Father and Mother closed their jaws tightly and knitted their eyebrows together as if to give it serious thought. (For they did not want to laugh at Rebecca's sincerity.) After careful thought, Father said that although it was a kind suggestion, he felt Grandma was a bit too old to play with dollies. No, they would have to think of something else.

Then Mother suggested since Grandma had a large backyard with nothing growing in it, that they buy a small fruit tree and plant it for her in her yard. That way, Grandma could see and enjoy their gift all year around.

Rebecca's eyes lit up with approval. She like the idea and again asked Father if she could go with him to buy the tree. Father nodded his head.

Rebecca, not really knowing what avocados were said, "I'm gonna find Gramma a blue one."

Father laughed and assured her that even though Grandma's favorite color was blue, he thought avocado trees probably only came in green.

Rebecca sat quietly with a puzzled look on her face, wondering why this tree only came in one color.

"Let's get this one," cried Rebecca. They had just arrived at the nursery and started to look, and already, Rebecca had chosen five trees to buy Grandma.

Finally, they found one about four and a half feet tall with a thick green stalk and shiny bronze-colored leaves. The root system was wrapped tightly in a plastic bag. And the tree looked very healthy.

They brought the tree home, and Father carefully carried it around to the backyard and leaned it against the garage in the shade. There, father said, it would be safe for a few days until they could take it over to surprise Grandma.

"Mama, Mama, come quick!" cried Rebecca. "Look at Gramma's tree. It's broked!"

Rebecca had gotten up early the following morning and had gone out to see the tree. And there, sure enough, lay the tree on its side—its main stock broken in half, branches split open, and leaves scattered all over the ground. Mother came running. When she saw the tree, she said a cat or dog had probably tried to climb up the branches and knocked it over.

When Father got home from work that evening, Rebecca ran to meet him, yelling and screaming, "Daddy! Daddy! Do you know what? Gramma's tree got broked. A dog and a cat tried to climb up it and broked it. Can we go buy Gramma another one? Can we, huh?"

Father went around to the backyard to see the tree with Rebecca following, asking the same question over and over. He knelt down to look closer; then holding the tree's stalk in his hand, he looked up at Rebecca and asked, "How much do you love Grandma?"

After a moment's thought, Rebecca, with arms stretched out wide, said, "I love Gramma this much!"

"Well, then," said Father, "we will not go and 'buy' Grandma another tree. But we shall do something really special to show Grandma that we love her. Tomorrow I'll come home early from work, and we will drive out into the country to a place that grows fruit trees for sale. And we shall dig one up for Grandma."

Rebecca was so excited that she ran and got her plastic shovel and put it on her pillow: still half-full with sand and a sand crab from the last beach adventure. The next day when Father got home, there was Rebecca waiting on the front porch with her shovel and bucket in one hand and Crystal her dolly in the other. The drive into the country was a long one, and Rebecca wondered if they would ever get there. The purple haze of late afternoon was beginning to deepen when they finally arrived at the grove.

They walked down row after row of trees until they came to a beautiful avocado tree about five feet tall and similar in color to the one that had been ruined.

"This one looks just right!" said Father.

Rebecca set Crystal up on a small rock next to the tree and started to push dirt onto her shovel. She was talking a blue streak by now to her dolly, to her father, even to an earthworm who had the unfortunate luck of being scooped up into her little shovel.

As her father dug around the tree, Rebecca talked. "Daddy, where do avocado trees come from?"

Father stopped digging and looked at his daughter. She had put down her shovel and was standing still, arms on hips, and waiting for an answer. "Rebecca," said Father softly, "Do you remember when Jesus said that unless a seed falls unto the ground and dies, it will live alone, but if the seed dies, it will grow up and bring forth much fruit? Well, inside of all kinds of fruit, there are little seeds. When a seed is planted in the ground, it stops being just a seed and begins to sprout a root. The root grows and is nourished by the dirt. Gradually, it will grow up to become a tree bearing new fruit so people can enjoy it. Inside of the new fruit are new seeds. When these new seeds are planted, new trees will grow from them too. This is the way God planned for people to have enough food to eat. Rebecca, do you know, too, that Jesus wants you to stop being just a little seed and to grow up to be something beautiful for Him, like this avocado tree?"

"Daddy, you mean if you put me this hole and throw dirt on my face, I will grow up and be a tree?"

Father laughed. "Well, no, not exactly," he said.

It was almost dark now. Father picked up the tree, and together, they slowly walked back to the car.

"No," continued Father. "Jesus is saying that if you will give up what you most want to have and what you most want to do, He will make you to be a person whose life will bless others. Like the avocado tree does when it stops being just a seed and grows to become a tree bearing fruit. It means to be willing, if necessary, to give up things that are important to you in order to make others happy. This is God's plan for you."

Father carefully put the little tree in the car and started back.

They were not yet halfway home before Rebecca made her discovery. "Daddy, I musa left Crystal at the tree place! Can you please go back and get her?"

Father turned the car around and headed back to the grove. But by the time they arrived, it was so dark they could only guess where the spot was where they had been digging. They looked and looked, down row after row of trees, but could not find Crystal!

After a long search, Father carefully explained to Rebecca that he thought Crystal was either probably covered by dirt or that someone had already picked her up. There was no use looking any more. Crystal was lost!

The long trip home this time was made even longer for Rebecca by the absence of her dolly. Slumped down in the back seat of the car, Rebecca sat very still with her chin buried in her chest and tears silently streaming down her cheeks. Sunken down with sorrow, Rebecca did not even hear father's gentle, consoling words spoken to her as they drove along. However, she was aware that something was poking her in the back of her head every time she moved. She reached up and back and felt something cool and soft. Then, suddenly, as if awakened from sleep, she whirled around to see the small upper limbs of the little avocado tree resting, like little hands, on her shoulders. And her tears for Crystal stopped.

The following day, as they drove to Grandma's, Rebecca was all smiles as she sat holding a large bag of potting soil on her lap. Today was the day they were going to plant Grandma's tree and surprise her.

Rebecca squatted down and watched very closely as father dug a deep hole and placed the little tree in the center and packed dirt tightly around the roots. "Can I put some potting soil in now, Daddy?" Rebecca asked, holding out a small handful of potting soil.

"Yes," said Father, "now is the time for the potting soil to be added."

When they had finished packing the dirt around the tree, Father made a little fence out of chicken wire and placed it over the tree to protect it from Gramma's dog and cats. Lastly, Mother took a clothespin and clipped a large birthday card to the wire fence. Now, all was ready. Father said Grandma would be out until way after dark and would probably not notice the tree until morning.

So Rebecca and her father and mother went home to wait for Grandma's phone call the next morning.

"I'll get it! It's Gramma!" yelled Rebecca, running to the phone the next morning. Father and Mother too hurried to get on the extensions.

"Happy birthday, Gramma! Gramma, do you know how we got your tree? Cuz I loss Crystal!"

Rebecca listed to Grandma. Then again she said, "Cuz I gave up my dolly, but it's okay cuz you more 'portant! Are you happy, Gramma?"

Putting the extension down, Father stood beaming at his daughter and listened to her understanding of a very hard lesson. And he wondered too at the wisdom of the great God, Who chose to reveal the goodness of His truths to even this youngest of hearts and in the simplest of ways—even in planting a tree for Gramma!

Planting a Tree, For Gramma

Did you find the 'DOVE' in the Tale?

Planting a Tree
for Gramma

BEe GOODness: The Adventures of Ritchie, the Beekeeper

"Miss Barton! Miss Barton! Come quick! Hornsby's at it again."

There in the corner of the dining room was the youngest boy in the orphanage. He had made a cup from a napkin then had poured honey into it and was trying to stuff the whole thing into his pocket when Miss Barton rushed across the room, stopping him just in time.

Ritchie and his father stood in the doorway, laughing at the party-like scene. He could see from the uncleared dinner dishes that the children had put his honey on their biscuits and had also buttered it on their fingers. Komal and Mary William, the newest twins to arrive, were busily slicking down a stray tomcat that had made the orphanage his home—fingers of honey and fur gracing their tongues between strokes, meows, and much laughter. And of course, there was Hornsby, gathering up for a late night treat.

Ritchie leaned over to his father and whispered, "Dad, I didn't think they would like my honey this much. It kinda makes me feel good. I'm glad I got the bees."

"Yes, son," said his father. "And from the looks of things, they have discovered some new ways of using the honey too, especially Hornsby."

Just then the door slammed shut at the end of a long dark hallway leading from the dining room. Windows rattled from the slam; and everyone, startled by the noise, sat very quiet, staring at the darkened corridor.

Nothing at first. Then a shadow. Until finally there appeared in full view a boy about twelve years old with fiery red hair. He shielded his eyes from the light of the dining room. Then, looking around, as if accounting for each child, his eyes slowly took in the whole scene until at last he saw Ritchie standing in the doorway. Suddenly, his arms went down stiff at his sides. His face flushed as red as his hair. And with fists clenched, he walked slowly toward Ritchie.

"Oh! Oh! The party's over," mumbled Ritchie, as he leaned closer to tell his father. "That's him, Dad! That's Buster. His eye is still swollen from the bee stings."

He took a step closer to his father because this was not the first time he had seen this look. Four months earlier, Ritchie had seen the same sneer on Buster's face and remembered his promises to get even. It was during a late afternoon practice scrimmage with his team that Ritchie first encountered Buster...

"Throw the ball! Throw it," yelled Ritchie.

Sonny Dale let go a perfect pass, and the football sailed in and then out of Ritchie's hands.

"Yuh shoulda had that one, Ritchie," yelled Billy.

"Ya shoulda had that one, kid. Maybe next time try using a butterfly net."

Everyone turned their heads to look at the uninvited spectator.

There, just outside the schoolyard fence, he stood, with a look of contempt on his face—a boy with fiery red hair.

"Oh yeah, who asked you?" demanded Ritchie.

"Go on, get out of here," yelled the rest of the boys. Then they each picked up a dirt clod and threw it at him.

Redhead backed up and started to run away, dodging clouds of dirt. When the last one hit him on the neck, he turned around, and with fists clenched in the air, he threatened to get even.

"Who is he?" asked Ritchie. "Does anybody know him?"

"His name's Buster," said Tommy. "He lives at Miss Barton's orphanage 'cross town. They say he's been there 'bout seven years 'cuz nobody wants him.".

"He's a troublemaker all right," volunteered Billy.

"Yeah," said Sonny Dale, "he's always gett'n' in fights."

The rest of the boys lined up to continue the game. But Ritchie stood watching as Buster walked slowly away down the street.

The next day in school when he heard again of Miss Barton's orphanage, Ritchie swallowed hard, and his thoughts went immediately to Buster. His teacher was discussing a class project to collect special food and toys for the children at the orphanage for Christmas. Everyone seemed very enthusiastic. But while they were busy thinking of ways they could contribute to the project, Ritchie could only think about Buster and his promise to get even. By the time class was over, however, Ritchie had made up his mind to do all he could for the kids at the orphanage—Buster or no Buster!

While he thought for days and days about his participation, it wasn't until his uncle's offer that Ritchie began his adventure as a beekeeper. Since there were still four months until Christmas, Ritchie's uncle suggested that if he started with two colonies of bees and worked very hard, he would have a sweet gift of honey to offer the children by Christmas.

"But won't I get stung, Unc?" asked Ritchie eagerly. "No," said his uncle, "not if you always follow these simple rules. Whenever you are working with your bees, always move very slowly and make sure you wear gloves and tuck your pants inside of your boots. That way, no bees will be able to climb up your trouser legs or crawl up the sleeves of your jacket."

"I'll remember!" said Ritchie. "What else?"

"Well, when it begins to get colder, you will need to make sure the hives are kept warm, at about 93 degrees. Take some burlap or canvas and drape it over the hives, leaving a small opening for the bees to go in and out. When the time comes, Ritchie, I will show you how to harvest the honey from the combs made by your bees. We will keep replacing the frames of combs filled with honey with empty ones. That way the bees will continue to fill up the waxy combs as long as they are able to find more nectar and pollen from surrounding trees and plants.".

"Boy, Unc, those bees sure do work hard, don't they?"

"Yes, Ritchie. They really are good little creatures. You must always treat them with respect."

Excited by his school project, Ritchie worked very hard for the next few weeks to get his bee colonies producing. He would come home after school, sometimes even missing football practice, in order to care for his bees. And in his spare time, he was usually found at the library or online, reading everything he could find on beekeeping.

Eventually, with his uncle's guidance, Ritchie's bee colonies began producing, at first small amounts of honey, then larger and larger amounts, until by Christmas, Ritchie had harvested over six quarts of honey. He stored the honey in glass jars kept in the garage until he could take it, along with all the other gifts his class had collected, to the orphanage.

The day of the party was a joyful one at the orphanage. All the children were surprised and delighted by the special gifts of clothing, food, and toys given by the other school's children.

It was hard to tell whether Ritchie was happiest when he proudly presented his two quarts of amber red honey to Miss Barton or whether he was even more happy because Buster was nowhere to be seen. He was glad Buster was not there to spoil the party. But he couldn't stop wondering where he was.

It was not until he got home that evening that Ritchie learned of Buster's whereabouts during the party. When Ritchie saw his beehives had been smashed and his beekeeping tools either broken or scattered over the yard, he didn't have to think twice about who had done these things.

He then ran to the garage only to find all but two quarts of the honey jars smashed to pieces and his bee netting cut to shreds. Yet, as he looked around at the mess, Ritchie felt it strange that he did not feel angry toward Buster. Even when he remembered his promise to get even, still, instead of feeling angry, Ritchie only felt sorry for him.

He slowly walked over to the last remaining jars of honey and carefully picked them up and carried them into his house.

Not knowing quite what to say and hoping to console his son, Ritchie's father said, "You know Ritchie, no one could have done this amount of damage without getting stung himself." He had no sooner said this when the phone rang.

"It's Miss Barton!" said his father. "It seems one of her boys came home with his eye badly swollen shut. She's inquiring about the condition of your beehives, Ritchie."

"'What color hair does he have?" asked Ritchie.

"Red!"

"It's Buster, Dad! He's the one that did it sure!"

Later that evening, after all the details were known, Ritchie asked his father if they could bring the remaining honey to the orphanage.

"Dad, I really want to give all my honey to Miss Barton's orphans. Besides, I need to settle something with Buster…"

Buster stood before him, ready to strike. But before he could say or do anything, Ritchie pushed two quarts of honey into his arms. A bit startled and a little embarrassed, Buster looked around once again at all the kids. It was then that this combination of a new gift of honey, the delight of the other children, and his still swollen eye became too much for him.

His scowl dissolved into a smile. And with head slightly bowed, he said, "Thanks for the honey, Ritchie. And I'm sorry for wreckin' your beehives."

As he turned to walk away, Ritchie caught him by the arm. "Hey, Buster, why don't cha come over to the school tomorrow and join our football team? We can always use a good receiver."

"Thanks, Ritchie. I think I will. Do you think I'll need my butterfly net?"

Both boys laughed and laughed. Afterwards, in the car going home, Ritchie's father said, "That was a fine thing you did just now, son, inviting Buster to join your team after what he did."

Ritchie, so deep in thought and not seeming to have heard his father's words, said, "Dad, why doesn't nobody want him?"

His father looked at him, and with his voice filled with regret, he explained. "Ritchie, it's because he's too old. People do not want to adopt kids Buster's age. But ya know, son, even though Buster may never have any parents, sometimes all that a guy may really need is a brother."

Ritchie thought for a few moments. Then, half to his father and half to himself, he murmured, "Boy, I hope he doesn't bring that butterfly net to practice tomorrow."

And Ritchie and his father laughed all the way home.

BEe GOODness: The Adventures of Ritchie, the Beekeeper

BEe GOODness: The Adventures of Ritchie, the Beekeeper

Did you find the 'DOVE' in the Tale?

A Penny a Can

How would he be able to earn the money needed in the next three weeks? Ernesto had just finished a long practice session and was there, alone on the bleachers, long after everyone had gone home. He sat with his chin cradled in his hands, thinking about opening day of the baseball season just three weeks away and how he had been chosen to pitch the first game for his team.

For a few moments, at least, he had felt very proud. But when Coach Dave mentioned the thirty dollars for uniform and registration fees, his heart sank. Ernesto did not have a part-time job. And he knew his mother did not have enough money to spend for anything extra, especially since she had just recently been able to buy him a new pair of long-overdue shoes for school.

Ernesto knew if he was going to be able to play Little League this year, he would have to raise the thirty dollars himself—and in a hurry too!

A few months earlier, Ernesto's friend Augie had told him about a job delivering newspapers after school. But when he applied for the job, Ernesto was told that he would need to supply his own bicycle. And since he did not have one, they could not consider him for the newspaper route. Ernesto stood up; picked up his glove and bat, and slowly began to walk home deep in thought for a way to earn thirty dollars.

Along the way back home he saw two men mowing their lawns, one beside the other, and he thought to himself, "That's it! Tomorrow after school, I will ask Alia Salazar if she will let me cut her grass. And maybe I can cut enough lawns to earn my uniform money and fees before the season begins.

Mrs. Salazar agreed. And so the next day, there was Ernesto, huffing and puffing behind a large lawnmower, trying to push it over a tough patch of Mrs. Salazar's crab grass. After about a half hour of huffing and puffing went by, Ernesto, seeing he had only mowed three feet of grass, suddenly ran home and got pair of his mother's sewing scissors. He then returned to cut Mrs. Salazar's lawn by hand.

When Mrs. Salazar came out and saw his patchwork effort, she smiled to herself. Then she gave Ernesto two quarters and told him that, while she appreciated his effort, she felt the work was a little too hard for him and that she would have someone else finish the lawn. Although Ernesto was disappointed, Alia Salazar had given him a good idea. Since he had to earn extra money, she recommended that he take peoples' dogs out for walks and exercise them for their owners. And that he might be able to start with Mr. Beatty's German shepherd, Champ!

"Here, Champ! Here, Champ! Here boy! Come back here!" yelled Ernesto. They had no sooner reached the sidewalk, when the leash broke loose from Ernesto's grip and Champ went tearing up the street after Mrs. Twillinger's pet Siamese cat. He chased the cat up a tree and stood leaning up against the trunk, barking and scratching.

Ernesto finally caught up to him, with Mr. Beatty and Mrs. Twillinger running close behind, yelling at each other's pet.

When news of this incident spread around the neighborhood, Ernesto's dog walking service came to an abrupt end. However, he had learned a valuable lesson. He learned he must not try to do jobs that were either too big or too heavy for him. (Champ had proved this to him in two short minutes.)

By this time, Ernesto was getting desperate. His daydreams of pitching a no-hitter on opening day gave way to concern over whether he would even be allowed to play at all. He then thought of a job to earn money that was neither too big nor too heavy for him to do. (After all, it only involved holding a garden hose and a sponge and bucket.)

He went and asked Mr. Hernandez if he could wash his new car. But by this time, Ernesto's reputation preceded him. Mr. Hernandez told him his car didn't need washing even though it was dirty. However, Augie's mother, Mrs. Tudesco, knowing his need for a job, allowed Ernesto to wash her car when he asked.

Everything was coming along just fine. Ernest was confident there would be no mistakes or damage done this time. He hosed off all the surface dirt, and he had just started to sponge clean the hood and fender of the car when Mrs. Tudesco came running out of her house, yelling, "Erneessttooo, watch out! The wwwwwiiiinnnnddddoooowwws!"

Startled by the screams, Ernesto turned around to face her, and as he did, the full force of the water hose stream was directed at Mr. Beatty, who had just stepped out onto his porch with Champ. The water hit Mr. Beatty with enough force causing him to slip on the steps and fall. As he was falling, he let go of the leash, and Champ took off again like a shot, after Mrs. Twillinger's cat, chasing her up the street.

With head hung low, Ernesto slowly walked toward the beachfront, thinking how foolish he had been to try to wash a car with the windows rolled down. (They said it would take about a week for the cloth upholstery to dry out.)

It now seemed hopeless that he would play Little League this year. Three days had already been wasted, and he had only managed to earn $1.50. Mrs. Salazar had paid him fifty cents for the yard work. And Mr. Beatty had given him a dollar if he promised to never go near his property or dog again.

As he neared the beach, he picked up an aluminum can off the sidewalk. He tossed it up and down once or twice in his hand and then threw a perfect strike at a trash container twenty feet away.

"Hey, don't do that! Don't you know those things are valuable?"

Ernesto turned around to see who was speaking. But before he could, she was already past him and bent over and down into the trash container, her legs and army boots flailing ferociously in the wind, then upside down, stretching her four-foot, one-inch body full tilt, trying to retrieve the can. Walking back toward him carrying the trash bag partially full of cans, the little white-haired woman was still admonishing him as she opened her bag to store the prize retrieved from the bottom of the trash container.

She told him there was a place that paid one penny for every aluminum can turned in. She also told him that if he wanted to earn his League money, he would need to collect about two hundred cans a day.

Ernesto felt this to be more than he could do when the little white-haired woman assured him that cans were very plentiful, but that many people were collecting them. Ernesto's eyes lit up. He liked competition. And he asked the woman to show him where to look and what to look for. As they searched, she carefully explained to him how and where to look for aluminum cans and even gave him a profile of the local competition.

As they walked from container to container, the little white-haired woman suddenly leaned over and whispered, "Don't say anything to her, but watch."

Coming toward them was a very small woman with slightly stooped shoulders and a deeply lined, swarthy face, pulling a small cart of aluminum cans behind her. As she came closer, Ernesto could see that her face and mouth seemed to be frozen in a constant scowl. She walked past them and never looked up but continued to stare vacantly at the sidewalk.

"She always does that," said the whitehaired woman. "She never says hello to anyone. I've watched her."

Just then a young boy appeared from a side street, pushing a large shopping cart. When he saw the white-haired woman, he stopped, and a look of total horror spread across his face. From his expression, Ernesto guessed that he knew the woman. And, when he saw her nostrils begin to flare and her feet pawing the good earth like a half-crazed snorting raging bull, Ernesto guessed the little white-haired woman knew the boy as well.

He pushed his cart one container ahead of us, all the time looking back with terror over his shoulder at the woman. A little faster. Then a little faster still we walked until finally, the little white-haired woman took off at a gallop, as if trying to win the

Kentucky Derby—both of them, neck and neck, racing the other to the next trash can finish line.

For the next week, Ernesto was up every morning very early, hunting for the cans he would need to buy his uniform. He saw the white-haired woman in close sprints with the little boy a few more times. And occasionally, near dark, he would see the little old woman pulling her cart with a few cans in it, slowly making her way up the boardwalk.

Ernesto felt very sad for this old woman. When he told his mother about her, he was surprised to learn that she knew who the old woman was. And, quite possibly, why she acted the way she did.

Ernesto's mother said the old woman's name was Mrs. Venable. She went on and explained to him, that she and some friends from their church had once taken food to Mrs. Venable because she was very poor. It was even rumored that she didn't have money for any food at all.

"Possibly this is the reason Mrs. Venable acts the way she goes," said his mother. "And why she also needs to collect aluminum cans."

Ernesto stood with his mouth wide open, listening to his mother's explanation.

The next afternoon, he loaded up his wagon with four large bags of aluminum cans he had collected and headed down to the beachfront to wait. He didn't have to wait very long before he saw the old woman step up onto the boardwalk with her small cart and begin to slowly walk toward him, looking in every trash container she came to.

He pulled his wagon up to meet her and whispered, "Mrs. Venable, I would like you to have these." Before she could react, he had placed all four bags securely in her cart. The old woman looked up and smiled at Ernesto. She then nodded her head and continued on her way without ever speaking a word.

Ernesto stood for a long time motionless as he watched the old woman walk away into the sunset, like the Lone Ranger, pulling his cans behind her.

"Play ball!" the umpire shouted, signaling the end of opening day ceremonies and the beginning of the first game of the Little League season. Ernesto watched his team take the field. He was very excited about the game even though he could not be out there playing. And while he sat in the highest corner of the grandstands with his mother next to him, he thought about Mrs. Venable. And he was glad to have been able to share his cans with her. This thought helped remove some of the sting of missing the baseball season.

After all, there would be many other seasons to follow for him. And he knew he had been challenged to give up just this one. But as for Mrs. Venable, he thought, her challenge was one renewed day after day—to find enough to live on, at a penny a can.

A Penny A Can

Did you find the 'DOVE' in the Tale?

Did you find the 'DOVE' in the Tale?

ABOUT THE AUTHOR

Forced by illness to retire in 2015 from a thirty-two-year career in industrial sales, I now spend my time as a minister serving the saints at Laurel Bible Chapel in San Diego, California. My wife and I have been active in our fellowship's AWANA and Sunday school programs over the years and formerly with a puppet ministry to our children's Sunday school. I have tried to prioritize my retirement availability with a special emphasis on discipling young men. I devoted the last two decades writing a chapbook of poetry entitled *"...from Ploughing Akel Dama"* (cultivating our "field of blood," giving expression to the biblically Christian mind-set worldview as the only valid and truthful take on life) as well as frequently publishing, in prose form, homilies to this end over social media.

CPSIA information can be obtained
at www.ICGtesting.com
Printed in the USA
FSHW020841011218
53915FS